SILLY WONDERFUL YOU

Story by
Sherri Duskey Rinker

Illustrated by
Patrick McDonnell

Balzer + Bray
An Imprint of HarperCollinsPublishers

For family, love, humor—and faith
—S.D.R.

Balzer + Bray is an imprint of HarperCollins Publishers.

Silly Wonderful You

Text copyright © 2016 by Sherri Duskey Rinker

Illustrations copyright © 2016 by Patrick McDonnell

www.harpercollinschildrens.com

———————————————

ISBN 978-0-06-227105-1

———————————————

The artist used pen, brush, and ink to create the illustrations for this book.

Typography by Jeff Schulz

16 17 18 19 PC 10 9 8 7 6 5 4 3 2

❖

First Edition

I never imagined,
before you came along . . .

that our house could get *this* messy and

Or that you'd be so silly,
and giggly,
and **splashy,**

and CRASHY!

jumpy.

could be

That you

so

Or sometimes
GRUMPY

(and maybe just a tiny bit whiny).

Or **stinky!**

(Phew! What do we feed you?!)

Or **slimy,**

and **grimy,**

And now . . .

since there was you . . .

my days start oh-so-early,
    with bright-eyed alarm clocks. . . .

Each time I step, sharp little blocks
go *right* through my socks!

I find so many things
in unusual places.

And *you find* such awesomely cool hiding spaces!

About a **million** stuffed animals have moved in with you,

and you make *amazing* creations
with glitter and glue!

Since there was you, I'm always surprised

at how much *fun* you are,

and how

GINORMOUSLY

I love you.

Since there was you . . .

At the end of a
sloppy,
noisy,
sticky (*sometimes even **icky!***),
wiggly
play
day,

I'm so, so sleepy

from all the racing

and chasing

(and the washing-your-face-ing!).

So cuddle in tight . . .

it's almost good night. . . .

Dozy, eyes close-y . . .

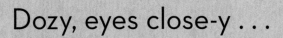

the day's almost through. . . .

I'm feeling SOOOOO tired....

(Aren't you tired, too?)

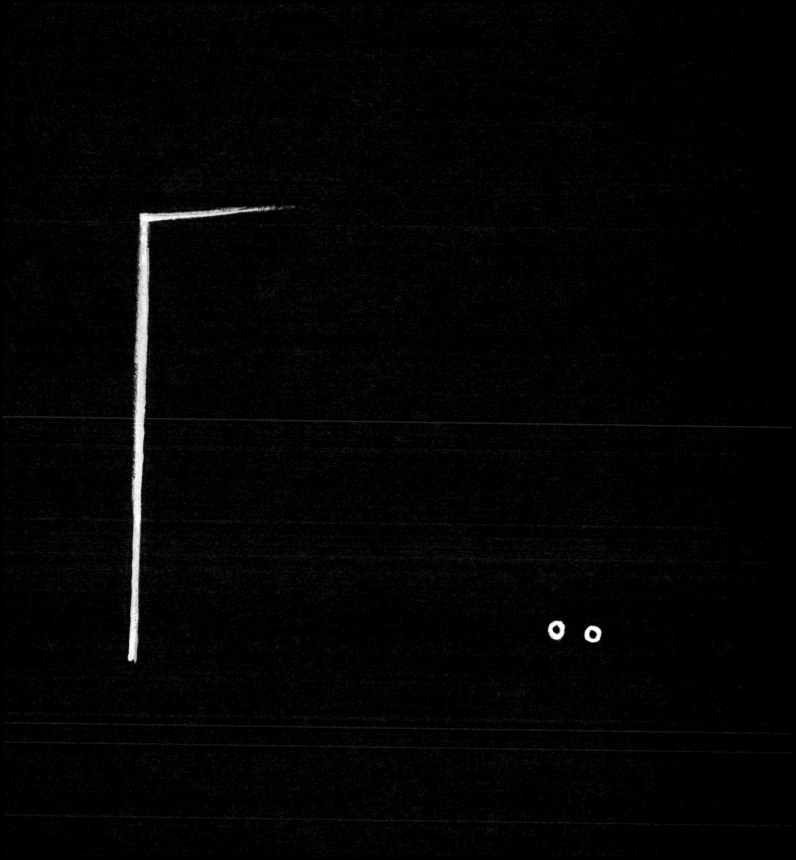

But since there was you,

I know now
that dreams really do
come true.